HANSEL, GRETEL

and the

DASTARDLY DINNER LADY

BY ISABEL THOMAS

ILLUSTRATED BY MÓNICA CARRETERO

Curious Fox

This story is based on the folk tale Hansel and Gretel. It was first written down by Jacob and Wilhelm Grimm (the Brothers Grimm) in 1812, but had been told by many storytellers before. Brother and sister Hansel and Gretel are abandoned in a forest by their wicked stepmother. A bird leads them to a little house made of bread, cake, and sugar. A little old lady invites them inside. At first she pretends to be friendly, but she is really a wicked witch who wants to eat them.

The witch locks Hansel in a cage and forces Gretel to cook meals to fatten him up. At first Hansel tricks the witch into thinking he is not fat enough to eat. But the witch gets impatient and decides to cook him anyway. She asks Gretel to check that the oven is hot enough, but Gretel tricks the witch into climbing into the oven herself. The children escape.

First published in 2015 by Curious Fox,
an imprint of Capstone Global Library Limited,
264 Banbury Road, Oxford, OX2 7DY
Registered company number: 6695582

www.curious-fox.com

Text copyright © Isabel Thomas 2015
Illustrations by Mónica Carretero

ISBN 978 1 782 02313 5

19 18 17 16 15
10 9 8 7 6 5 4 3 2 1

A CIP catalogue for this book is available from the British Library.

Printed and bound in China.

For Zachary Merlin Jones

Hansel

Gretel

Mrs Maggot, the
Dinner Lady

Hungry Children

Rat

Hansel and Gretel would do anything for pudding.

Unfortunately, their dinner lady only gave pudding to children who cleared their plates.

Mrs Maggot's dinners were so disgusting, no one EVER got to taste the treats from the pudding trolley.

Hansel and Gretel tried hiding their horrid dinners, but Mrs Maggot had a knack for sniffing out leftovers.

"Try that trick again, and I'll throw you in the bin," she snarled.

Hansel and Gretel gasped. Mrs Maggot's victims reeked of rotten food for weeks!

One day Hansel and Gretel came up
with a plan to get pudding.

They waited until Mrs Maggot was busy adding
cockroaches to the soup (for extra crunch).

Then Gretel crept
towards the trolley, and
poked a tiny hole in a
tub of chocolate sauce.

After school,
Hansel and Gretel
followed a trail of
chocolate drops
into the kitchen ...

... through a
cabbagey fog ...

... to a cupboard marked "KEEP OUT!!"
So, of course, they let themselves in.

Inside, they found every kind of pie, pudding and pastry in the world.

Let's eat!

Hansel and Gretel were on second helpings,
when they heard a voice behind them...

Hansel and Gretel were trapped.

Gretel stared at the mountain of mouldy washing-up and sighed. It would take HOURS.

Then she spotted a chicken bone. With a grin, she kicked it under the cupboard door.

Hansel grabbed the bone and
wiggled it around in the keyhole.
The door opened... but it was not
Gretel on the other side.

KEEP OUT !!

It was Mrs Maggot, turning as purple as her pigeon pie.

"Open the bin," she barked. "That beastly boy is going in."

Gretel climbed the steps to the stinking bin.
She knew the dinner lady would push her in too.
So Gretel huffed, and she puffed, and she said quietly,

"I can't lift the lid."

Mrs Maggot climbed the steps and threw the lid open quickly.

Too quickly.

The dinner lady WIBBLED, and WOBBLED, and TOPPLED in headfirst.

"We're free!"
cried Hansel.

"Free to eat pudding!"
grinned Gretel.

And as for Mrs Maggot,
she got closer to her
school dinners than
anyone had ever dared.